Belon[illegible]
Sabrina Surace

Riding Silver Star

JOANNA COLE

Photographs by MARGARET MILLER

Morrow Junior Books • New York

Photographer's Note

First and foremost, I want to thank rider Aubrey Cohen for her endless patience and enthusiasm, her natural composure in front of a camera, and her friendship. "Brie" is a true star. Kelly Hoy, her superb teacher, graciously opened her stable doors to this project. Mirabelle Dickhart, Brie's mother, was constantly helpful, and Alan Cohen, her father, truly saved the day on more than one occasion. The New Canaan Mounted Troop was terrific, especially Janice Elmore and Michelle Schmerzler. Thanks also to troop members Kelly Elmore, Greg Parrett, Jessie Caird, Emily Baldwin, and Jill Frankel.

The text type is 15.5-point Dutch 823.

Inquiries should be addressed to William Morrow and Company, Inc.,
1350 Avenue of the Americas, New York, NY 10019.
Printed in Singapore at Tien Wah Press.
1 2 3 4 5 6 7 8 9 10

Library of Congress Cataloging-in-Publication Data
Cole, Joanna.
Riding Silver Star/by Joanna Cole; photographs by Margaret Miller.
p. cm.
ISBN 0-688-13895-0 (trade)—ISBN 0-688-13896-9 (library)
1. Horsemanship—Juvenile literature. 2. Show riding—Juvenile literature.
[1. Horsemanship. 2. Show riding.] I. Miller, Margaret, ill. II. Title.
SF309.2.C64 1996 798.2'5—dc20 95-13268 CIP AC

To Rachel,
my horsegirl
—J.C.

For Tyke,
my riding teacher
and friend
—M.M.

Silver Star is my horse. I call him Star for short. My name is Abigail. My friends call *me* Abby for short. I have to hurry to get ready for my riding lesson. My teacher won't like it if I'm late.

First I have to brush Star so his coat is shiny.

His hooves need cleaning, too. I make sure no stones are stuck there. That could hurt.

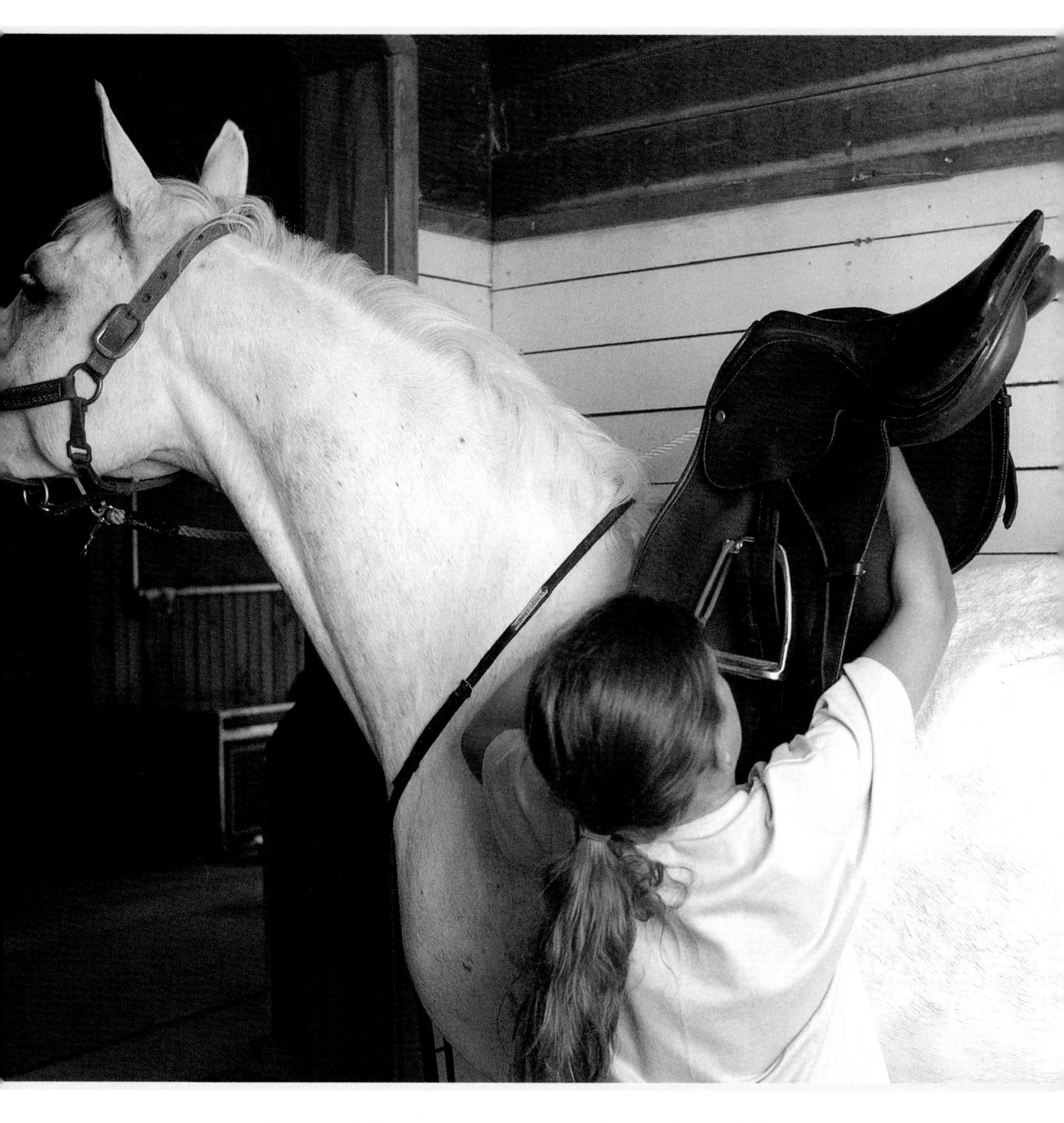

The saddle goes on top of a soft saddle pad.

If I don't tighten the girth enough, the saddle might slip to the side while I'm riding. I'd go with it, and that's no fun!

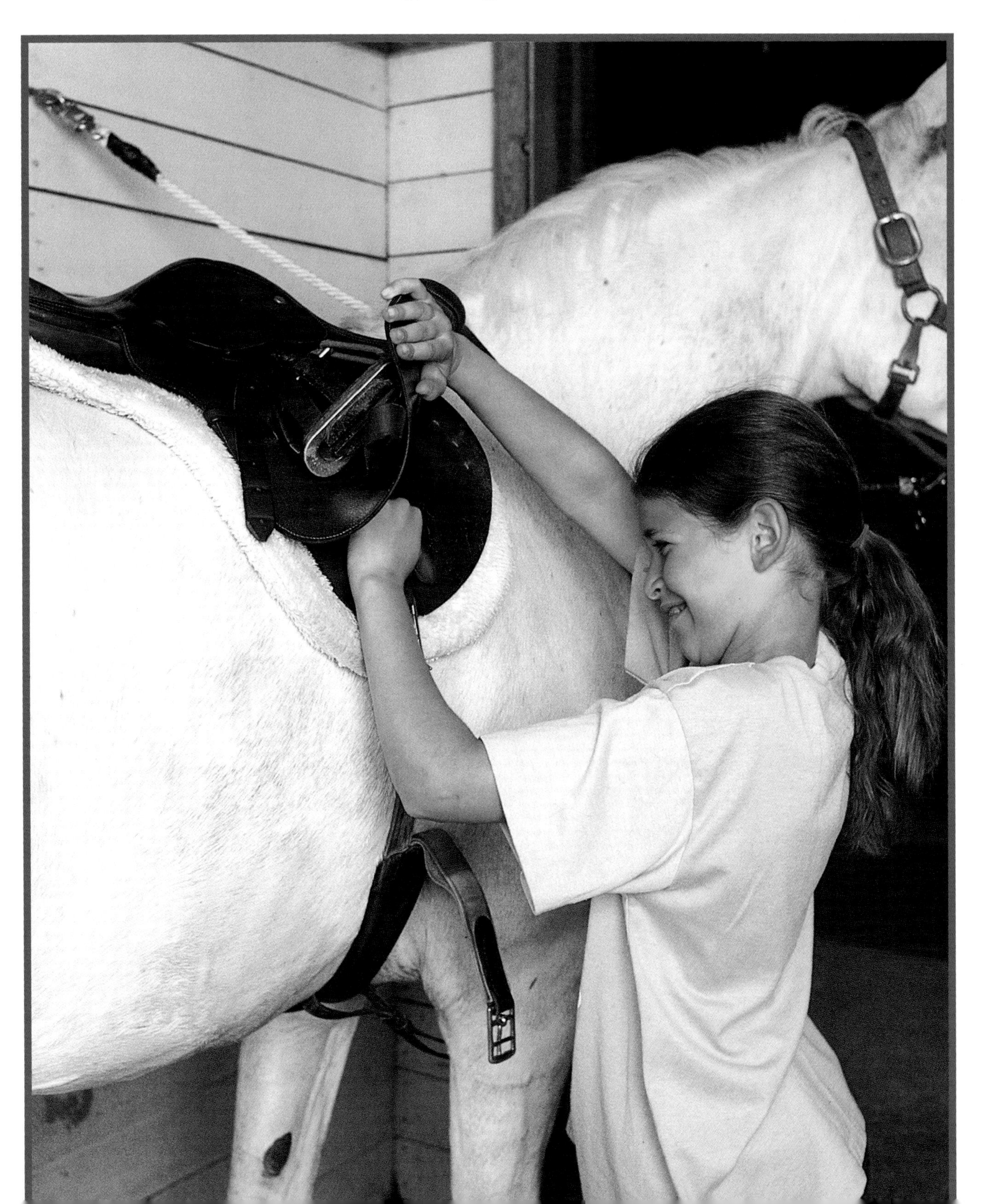

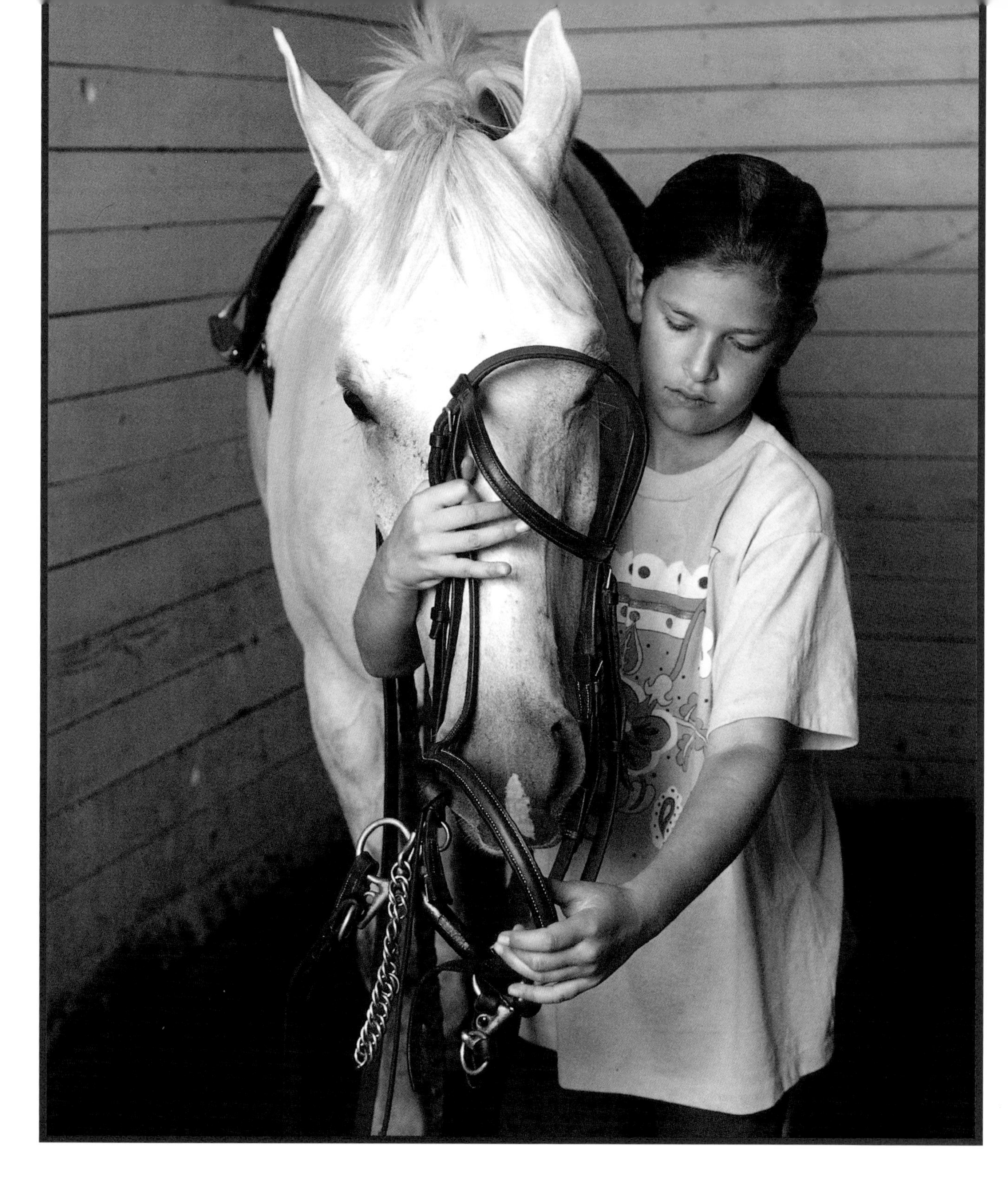

The final thing Star needs is his bridle. The metal bit goes between his teeth, and the reins are attached to it. That's how I "steer" him.

Now it's *my* turn to get ready. I need leather pants to get a good grip with my legs. I need boots to fit snugly in the stirrups. And I need a hard hat to protect my head in case I fall. I hope I won't!

Now Star is ready, and I am ready. Marilyn, the dog, jumps up to wish me good luck.

Star is so tall, I need to climb up on a mounting block to get in the saddle.

"Hi, Ellen," I say to my teacher. "We're ready!" I'm hoping to get a ribbon in the horse show next week, so we need to work hard.

First we have to practice some fancy footwork.

Then it's time to jump fences. I try to remember to ride the way Ellen taught me: back straight, chin up, heels down, hands forward. I use the reins and my legs to tell the horse what to do. It's hard to remember everything at once.

I give Star a squeeze with my legs to tell him, *Jump now!* We go over, but I'm too far back in the saddle. I'm supposed to be leaning forward so Star and I will go over together. But this time I got left behind.

Ellen shows me the right way and tells me to try again.

Here we go. I start out forward. So far, so good....

Thank goodness—I stay forward, and I finish forward. I remember to keep my heels down. Star did everything right, too. Hooray!

"You did a great job, Abby," says Ellen.

I tell Star he did a great job also.

The whole lesson lasts about an hour. After all that work, Star is hot and sweaty.

I give him a cool bath.

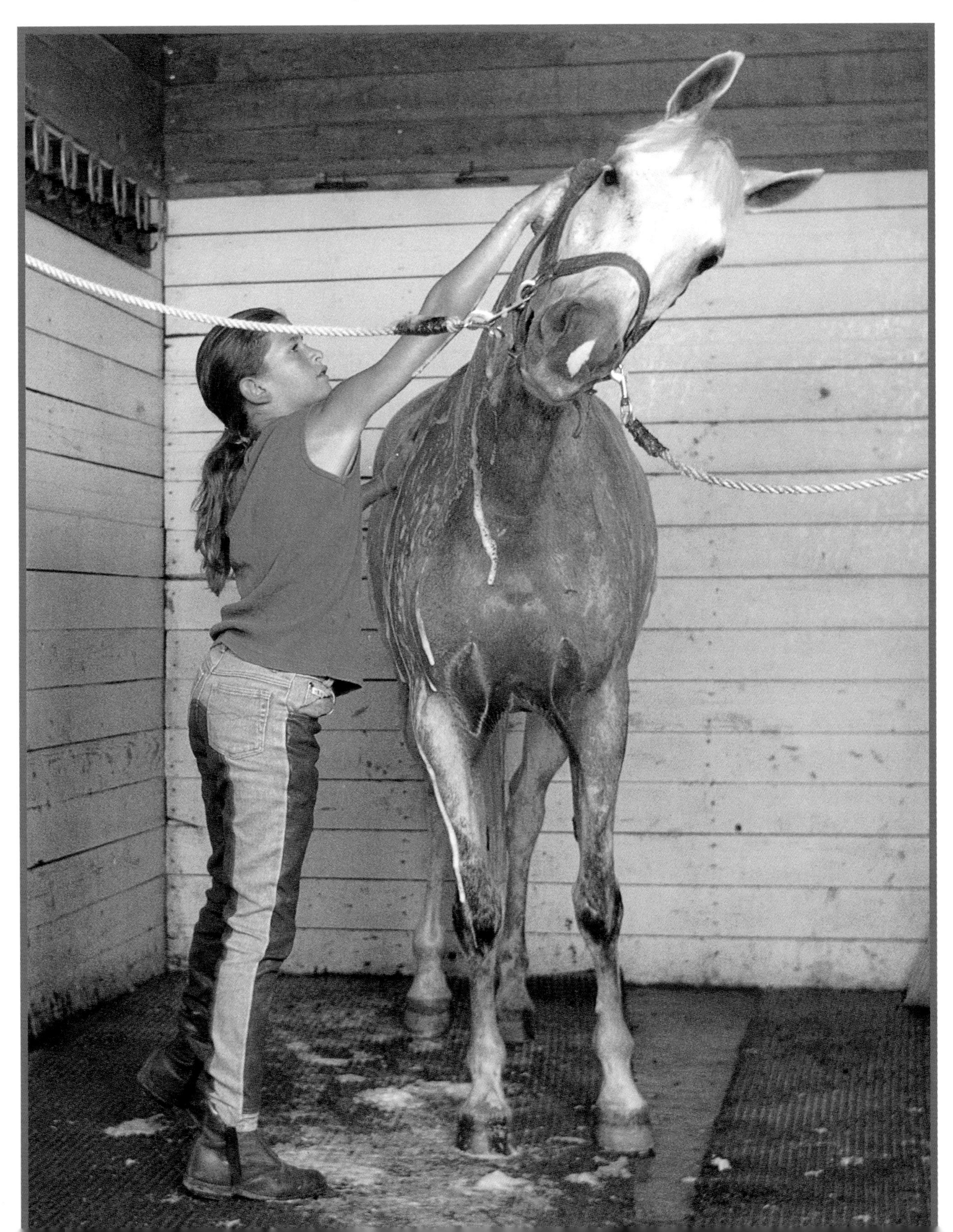

Then he needs a walk in the sun to dry off. If I put him in the barn while he's still wet, he might get sick.

Now Star has to rest. I clean up his stall for him.

Then I give him water, grain, and a pile of fresh hay to eat.

Star is happy in his stall, and I'm ready to go home. Marilyn gives me a lick. She seems to be saying, Congratulations—it was a great lesson.

The next time I come to the stable, Ellen and I go on a trail ride. We ride past farms and into the woods.

It's fun to leave the stable behind and see new things. Star isn't used to walking through water, and he watches it splash.

All of a sudden we hear kids calling my name. Some of my friends are out for a trail ride, too. We all ride together. Meg and I will both be going to the horse show. We talk about how excited we are.

When we stop for lunch, I give Star my apple.
Maybe that wasn't such a good idea....

He wants more, and it's hard to say no
to a 900-pound pet!

On the way back, Ellen says, “Let’s race!”

She had a head start, but Star catches up.

Up ahead we see a good fence for jumping. I shout, “First one over the fence wins!” I give Star a squeeze, and…

we're over first! Hooray, we won!

At last, it's time to go to the horse show. Star has to ride in a horse trailer. At first, he doesn't want to. But before long, we're on our way.

Everything's exciting at the show. Meg and I walk around, taking it all in. The horses are spick-and-span, and the riders have on their best show clothes.

I watch other riders competing for ribbons. Then it's my turn.

Over the loudspeaker, I hear: "Silver Star, ridden by Abigail Allen." I ride into the ring. I look fine on the *outside,* but *inside,* boy, am I nervous!

Now it's time to show what we've learned. Back straight, chin up, heels down, hands forward. I remember everything!

I lean forward. With my legs, I tell Star when to jump.
It's perfect—we go over together!

We did such a good job, we got a ribbon…

but Star likes orange soda better!

It was fun to show and fun to win, but the most fun of all is just riding Silver Star.